Ciara.

Rusty

This series is for my riding friend Shelley,
who cares about all animals.

Visit the Animal Magic website:
www.animalmagicrescue.net

STRIPES PUBLISHING
An imprint of Magi Publications
1 The Coda Centre, 189 Munster Road, London SW6 6AW

A paperback original
First published in Great Britain in 2007

Text copyright © Jenny Oldfield, 2007
Illustrations copyright © Sharon Rentta, 2007
Cover illustration copyright © Simon Mendez, 2007

ISBN: 978-1-84715-022-6

A CIP catalogue record for this book is available from the British Library.

Printed and bound in Belgium

2 4 6 8 10 9 7 5 3

Rusty

Tina Nolan
Illustrated by Sharon Rentta

stripes

ANIMAL MAGIC
Meet the animals

Visit our website at
www.animalmagicrescue.net

Working our
magic to match
the perfect pet
with the perfect
owner!

GORDON
A gorgeous black and
white goat. He's sleek and
silky and very smart!
Good company for
ponies out at grass.

ROSA AND TULIP
Friendly, playful and
affectionate kittens, would
like homing together.
Aren't they adorable?

STELLA, TIMMY AND RINGO
This hand-reared trio is ready
to go! Stella loves a cuddle,
Timmy is a shy little thing and
Ringo has a twinkle in his eye.

RESCUE CENTRE

in need of a home!

JASPER
Jasper is a three-year-old
brown and white terrier
who would love a new
home in the country.
Lively and loveable.

PETAL
An unwanted Easter
bunny with beautiful black
and white markings.
Could you love her
all year round?

MILLIE
Millie's life has been hard
but even so she is patient
and kind. Can you give her
the home she deserves?

SAM
Sam is loyal and
dependable. He needs
a gentle owner with lots
of love to give.

Chapter One

"Gordon is a black and white goat," Karl Harrison typed. "He needs a home with high fences and plenty of grass."

"Put 'gorgeous' in front of 'black and white'," Eva told him. "'A gorgeous black and white goat'. We have to make people really want to adopt him!"

"OK," Karl muttered. "G-o-r-g-e-o-u-s." He'd already scanned a picture of Gordon into the computer. Now it was up to him and Eva to write a description.

"What else? Can we say he's great with ponies and horses?"

"Good idea. How about, 'Good company for ponies out at grass'. That should make horsey people look twice."

As Eva and Karl worked at the computer in Reception at Animal Magic Rescue Centre, their mum, Heidi, was busy in the surgery next door. She was admitting a young, abandoned terrier called Jasper.

"Just look at this poor dog's teeth!" Heidi tutted.

Joel, the centre's assistant, peered into the terrier's mouth.

"See! There's a build up of plaque and gum disease like you'd never believe," Heidi complained. "And Jasper can't be more than three or four years old."

Joel nodded. "I can see. It won't be long before his teeth begin to drop out."

"Not if I have anything to do with it," Heidi said firmly. "Let's microchip him and give him his jabs, then get straight to work on some dental hygiene before it's too late!"

But the little white and brown dog had other ideas. When they tried to look into his mouth again, he squirmed and wriggled, yelped and barked.

"Calm down," Joel said. "We're trying to help here."

"Woof!" Jasper objected. "Woof! Woof!"

"Hey, do you mind – I can't hear myself think!" Karl objected. "What else can we say about Gordon?" he asked Eva. "Come on, you're good at these description thingies."

"OK. 'Gordon is a gorgeous black and white goat'," she repeated. "'He's sleek and silky and very smart!'"

From the moment their dad had brought Gordon into the rescue centre the day before yesterday, Eva had adored him.

"The owners can't handle him any more," Mark had explained. "They say he eats everything in sight and has escaped from his field more times than Houdini!"

Heidi had shaken her head and sighed. "He's going to be a hard one to rehome," she'd predicted. "These days, people want nice, quiet ponies and donkeys, not noisy goats. Especially a billy goat."

But Eva had fallen in love the moment Gordon trotted into the stable. "He's gorgeous!" she'd sighed, putting her arms around his neck and letting him nuzzle close. "How could anyone possibly not want someone as adorable as Gordon!"

"Dad, why don't people want goats?" Eva asked.

She'd left Karl in Reception, hard at work on the computer. Crossing the yard, she found her dad mucking out the new stables. It was early evening. The sun was setting over the golf course beyond the river at the back of Animal Magic.

"Because goats are greedy, noisy and famously bad tempered." Her dad grinned, and winked at her as he wheeled a barrow out of the stable block.

"Hush!" Eva looked astonished. "Don't say that. Gordon can hear you!"

Her dad laughed. "He doesn't understand – he's a goat, remember!"

"Goats are clever," she protested, blocking his way. "For all we know, Gordon can understand every word you say!"

"OK, Gordon, I didn't mean it!" Mark called over his shoulder. "I love you anyway!"

"You do?" Eva checked.

He nodded. "Even though he just butted me while I was mucking out his stall."

"Really?"

"Really! Right on my backside – pow!" Gingerly Mark rubbed the spot.

"Oh – I'm sure he didn't mean to," Eva said hastily. Now she wanted to get past her dad to check on Gordon and make sure he hadn't hurt himself. She sidestepped and slipped into the stables.

"He meant it all right," Mark muttered, as he wheeled the barrow across the yard. "And I have the bruises to prove it!"

"I love you, Gordon!" Eva soothed the goat's hurt feelings. She noted the full hay-net and the bucket of fresh green cabbage leaves in the corner of his stall.

"And so does Dad. He's given you all this yummy food!"

Gordon nuzzled close to Eva. His dark brown eyes were fringed with lush white lashes. His black face had two beautiful white stripes running down its length.

"You're so silky smooth," Eva murmured. She stroked his neck, then bent to pick a choice cabbage leaf from the bucket.

With perfect timing, Gordon lowered his head and gently butted her in the back. Eva pitched forward into the newly laid straw.

"Hey!" she cried. "I've just been sticking up for you and now you go and do that!"

Picking herself up, she glanced round at Gordon, who stared at her with twinkling eyes. The corners of his mouth were turned up in what Eva could have sworn was a smile.

"Gordon!" she cried. "You're wicked!"

He flicked his long white ears and did a little hop and skip in the straw.

"But you're still my favourite!" Eva grinned. "Whatever people say about you, you're still totally ... well, wicked is all I can say!"

Chapter Two

Eva bolted the door of the stable block, then set off across the yard. An owl roosting in the trees beyond the golf course hooted in the twilight.

"Dad, did you check the side gate?" she called across the yard. There was no answer, so she decided to do it herself. Checking the gate was part of the evening routine at Animal Magic. Often people dumped their unwanted pets there just as it was growing dark.

Sometimes there would be a note Sellotaped to a cardboard box – 'Her name is Molly. She's eight weeks old. Please take care of her.' And inside the box there would be a lonely, frightened puppy.

But most of the time there was no note, no explanation – nothing except an abandoned cat in a basket, or a shivering pet rabbit, sometimes even a snake, and once, earlier in the summer, a bright red and blue macaw, complete with cage.

Eva opened the side gate that led out on to a narrow lane. She looked up and down. Tonight there was nothing to see, but as she went to close the gate she heard something – a faint noise carrying on the breeze. Eva went out into the lane and listened hard.

Perhaps she was wrong. What she'd thought was the cry of an animal in distress had probably been nothing after all. Once more she turned to close the gate.

Then she heard it again – a high-pitched call. It was definitely an animal, she was sure this time. The sound came from somewhere in the horses' field at the back of the rescue centre. Very high, very frightened and helpless.

Without stopping to think, Eva set off down the lane. She climbed the fence into the field where their next-door neighbour, Linda Brooks, kept Guinevere and Merlin the foal. She saw the mare standing alert at the top of the field, staring down the slope.

"It's OK, I'm on to it," Eva muttered to the two horses. She made her way quickly down the hill until a shout came from the Brookses' garden.

"Eva, what are you up to?" Linda Brooks

called. "It's going to be dark in a minute."

Trust Linda to have her eagle eye on the field! Eva sighed, then trotted up the hill to explain. "I thought I heard something down by the fence."

"What kind of thing? Do you think thieves are trying to steal the horses? Wait here. I'll fetch Jason."

"No, wait!" Eva might have guessed that their nervy neighbour would jump to the wrong conclusion. "It's nothing like that. The sound I heard was like a small animal in distress – maybe a kitten or a puppy. Who knows, the poor thing might have been dumped outside our gate a while ago. Maybe it's made its way down towards the river."

"Oh, I see, you're on a rescue mission." Quickly Linda Brooks relaxed. "But are you sure you should go alone?"

"It's OK, honestly." Eva had no time to lose – the light was fading fast and the poor creature, whatever it was, was still crying out for help. "I'll be quick."

"Oh yes, I hear it!" Linda nodded. "I'll run next door and tell your mum and dad."

Escaping at last, Eva turned and sprinted down the hill. The noise drew her to the fence, where she stopped and knelt down on her hands and knees.

"Why does it have to be so dark?" she muttered, pushing through long grass. The cries had stopped, but she could hear movement in some low thorn bushes beyond the fence, on the sloping bank leading to the river. Eva crawled under the strong wooden fence towards the bushes.

"Oh!" she gasped.

To one side, she saw amber eyes flash in the dark shadows then vanish.

Eva ignored them as, down below, the high, frightened cry began again.

She crept on towards the sound, which was almost lost in the rushing water. She was a metre from the river, straining to hear. What tiny creature was it that had found itself in such danger?

Eva's foot sank into boggy ground and she almost lost her balance. The water raced by, fast and dangerous.

"Whoa, nearly!" she muttered, stooping again and parting the long grass by the river's edge.

The creature's cry was frantic. Eva saw another pair of bright eyes. She heard howls of pain. Reaching to rescue the small, trembling animal, she found that it was trapped by its leg in a short coil of rusty barbed wire.

What now? If she tugged at the wire, it would only cut deeper into the flesh. "Hush," she whispered. "Don't struggle. I'm here to help."

As the creature wriggled between her hands and cried, Eva made out a white flash of fur on its chest. Perhaps it was a puppy, though it was too dark to see clearly.

"Eva, where are you?" a voice yelled from the horses' field.

"Down here!" Eva recognized her mum's

voice. "By the river. I need help!"

"I'm on my way. Hold on."

"We'll soon get you free," Eva murmured, stroking the soft fur.

Then a torch beam raked through the bushes and Heidi appeared. "What have we got?" she asked as she climbed the fence and scrambled down the bank.

"I think it's a puppy." Eva held on as gently as she could. "He's got his leg caught in some barbed wire. We need to loosen it without hurting him any more."

"I'll use my fleece jacket," Heidi decided, quickly pulling the long sleeves over her hands to protect them. "Hold him still and shine the torch with your other hand. I've found the end of the wire. Now I'm going to unwind it from round his leg. That's right, Eva, you're doing a great job."

Eva winced as the creature cried. At last

her mum got rid of the tangled wire.

"Now let's take a proper look at you, you poor little thing," Heidi said.

"Oh, his leg's bleeding really badly!" Eva cried.

Her mum examined it quickly. "Looks like he's already lost a lot of blood. He's pretty weak."

"Quick, let's get him home!"

"Wait a minute, Eva. Can you shine the torch on his face?"

Eva did so. The beam of light picked out a brown face, a white muzzle and big, pointed ears tipped with black.

"This is no puppy," Heidi told Eva, studying the young creature.

"Let me see, Mum." Eva was torn between taking a close look and getting back to the surgery. She led the way up the bank and into the field.

"You've rescued a fox cub," her mother said, cradling the creature in her hands.

"Wow, I've never rescued one of those before!" Eva gasped.

"He's probably about six weeks old. And I'm sorry to tell you this, but at this moment I'd say his chances of survival are pretty slim."

"You mean he might die?" Eva gasped.

Her mum nodded.

As they ran up the hill, a pair of piercing bright eyes watched from the undergrowth.

"Come on, Mum, we have to hurry!" Eva cried. "He mustn't die. Not now – we can't let him!"

Chapter Three

"OK, I've stopped the bleeding and put five stitches in the leg wound." Back at the surgery, Heidi worked fast. Joel stood by with the tools she needed.

"We'll put him on a fluid drip overnight and check his temperature every hour. That way, we'll know whether any infection has got into the wound."

Eva hovered close by. The fox cub was tiny and weak. He lay on his side with his eyes almost shut, taking shallow breaths.

"Where will you put him?" she asked Joel, who was setting up the drip.

"In the kitten unit," Joel said quietly. "We'll use a heat lamp on him to keep him warm and cosy."

"Poor little thing!" Eva breathed. Her heart went out to the helpless baby. "Can I stay up and keep an eye on him?" she asked her mum.

Heidi shook her head. "That's Joel's job."

"But Joel will be too busy to sit with the cub all of the time. What if he suddenly gets worse?"

"Eva, you can't do any more than you've already done," Heidi insisted. "And you need your sleep. Come on. Let's go over to the house."

"But Mum!" Eva protested. The cub's high-pitched cries for help still rang in her ears. How could she possibly sleep, not knowing if he was going to pull through?

"Don't worry, Eva. I promise I'll look after him." Carefully Joel picked up the cub and carried him into the cattery. The door swung closed behind him.

"Let's go," Heidi said again.

Silently, her head hanging, Eva followed her mum across the yard and into the house.

"I'm going to call him Rusty," Eva told Joel. She'd been up with the lark and out in the cattery, still in her pyjamas, before anyone else was awake. Now she gazed anxiously at the tiny fox cub.

"Rusty suits him," Joel agreed.

The cub seemed to be breathing better and was fast asleep.

"How is he?" Eva held her breath and waited for Joel's answer. It was as if she'd held it all night, hardly sleeping, wondering how the fox cub was doing.

"He's holding his own," Joel said. "His temperature's normal. The wound is clean."

"So he's going to be OK?"

Joel let a few seconds go by before he replied. "Wait and see."

"Meaning?"

"Meaning – wait and see!" Joel smiled kindly. "Rusty is a fighter, I will say that."

As if to prove it, the little cub slowly opened his eyes and tried to raise his head. Weak as he was, he looked around him then pulled at the tube attaching him to his drip.

"OK, little fella, we can take this away now if it's annoying you." Swiftly Joel disconnected the tube.

"Well done, Rusty!" Eva breathed, bending over the unit. "You made it through the night!"

The cub looked up at her with his big, light brown eyes. They were flecked with sparks of gold.

"You're beautiful!" Eva whispered. "Your name is Rusty and you're going to be fine!"

"Hey, Eva, why are you still in your pyjamas?" Annie Brooks asked. She'd come straight to the house at nine o'clock, looking for Eva. Karl had told her to try the cattery.

"Why, what time is it?" Happily bottle-feeding a tabby kitten, Eva glanced up at her friend.

"Time you were dressed," Annie grinned. "Mum mentioned that she'd seen you in the field last night. She said you were on a rescue mission. What happened?"

Eva gently put Rosa the kitten back into her cosy unit. Rosa snuggled up to her brothers and sisters. "I'll show you," Eva said, her brown eyes sparkling as she led the way to Rusty. "This is what happened!"

"A baby fox!" Annie exclaimed, her own face lighting up with delight.

Rusty lay curled up, blinking sleepily. His little pink tongue peeped out of his mouth and he licked his lips.

"What's wrong with him? Where did you find him? Oh, he hurt his leg!" Words tumbled out of Annie's mouth.

"Ssshhh!" Eva warned. "Don't scare him."

Annie crouched level with Rusty and gazed at him through the clear sides of the unit. "I've never seen a fox this close before," she murmured. "He's amazing."

"And he's hungry," Joel interrupted, presenting Eva with a syringe filled with warm milk. "Here's a seat for you. Have a go at feeding him," he invited.

Nodding eagerly, Eva lifted Rusty on to her lap. He felt warm and soft. His pointy tail with its white tip brushed against her hand. "Do I give it to him the same way I do with the kittens?" she asked Joel.

"Yes, don't be scared. Just slide the dropper into his mouth and let the liquid trickle in."

Nervously Eva gave Rusty the milk, relaxing as the cub tasted the first drops then swallowed eagerly.

"Aah!" Annie sighed. "He's cute!"

Rusty gulped greedily until the syringe was empty.

"Phew!" Eva was relieved. "He can't be that ill," she grinned.

"No, there's nothing wrong with his appetite," Joel agreed. "Let's check his temperature and pulse."

The girls watched as Joel carried out the checks and then put Rusty back in the unit.

"Hmm," he murmured as he read the thermometer.

"What?" Eva and Annie asked.

"Temperature's a little high. It may be nothing to worry about though."

Just then, Karl hurried into the cattery. "Who says people don't like goats?" he cried, spying Joel, Eva and Annie gathered by Rusty's unit. "Hey – cute fox cub," he said casually.

"Ssshhh!" Eva said. "Don't frighten him."

Karl ignored her. "Anyway, I just got an email from a couple who want to take a look at Gordon! It's amazing – he's only been on the website for less than twenty-four hours!"

"Ssshhh!" Eva said again, dragging her brother down the row of cat bays then out into Reception. Annie sneaked one last look at Rusty then followed.

"Mr and Mrs Wesley want to give Gordon a home!" Karl insisted. "Mum was wrong – people *are* interested in goats. The Wesleys say Gordon would live in a field with their pony, who's a Welsh cob called Henry. How cool is that?"

"Very cool," Eva agreed. "When are they coming to see him?"

"It's Saturday, so they can come today," Karl crowed. "It's a record – we found a home for a goat in less than a day!"

Annie watched Karl and Eva do a high five by the Reception desk. "Aren't you counting your chickens before they're hatched?" she asked cautiously.

Eva frowned. Karl shook his head. "No way!" they both said.

"Watch it, Annie, you're starting to sound like your mum," Karl added, dashing off to find his dad and tell him the good news.

Chapter Four

"Yes, I'm afraid Rusty has developed a fever," Heidi told Eva and Annie later that morning. The latest temperature check had confirmed Joel's earlier suspicions.

"That's not good, is it?" Annie asked.

Eva crouched down to take a closer look at the cub.

"No, but it often happens when there's an open wound where the dirt can get in. However much we wash and clean it, there's still a risk."

"Will you give him antibiotics?" Eva asked anxiously. Rusty was lying on his side, his legs outstretched, his body limp.

Her mum nodded. "And plenty of fluid. He's just had a drink of water, so what we need to do now is leave him in peace."

"You heard that, Rusty? You have to stay here and rest," Eva whispered. Her heart sank at the latest news. Would this lonely, small creature find the strength to stay alive? "We'll look after you as best we can," she promised, leaving him to sleep.

"OK, Gordon, it's time for your beauty treatment," Eva said, peering into the goat's stable. The girls were armed with sprays, brushes and combs, and were doing their best to stay busy and not worry about Rusty.

Gordon glanced out over his stable door. He snickered when he spotted the brushes.

"We have to make you look good for your visitors," Eva explained. "You're a handsome boy and you need to impress Mr and Mrs Wesley by looking your best."

"He's a goat," Annie pointed out. "He doesn't understand."

"Yeah, that's what Dad thought, but he managed to hurt Gordon's feelings all the same. Gordon's dead clever, aren't you, boy?" Eva opened the stable door and went in. Annie followed close behind.

The goat stepped back to take a good look at the girls. He rolled his yellow eyes at the white plastic bottle which Eva held in her hand.

"It's de-tangler and conditioner," she explained. "I spray it on your coat, like so."

Squirt-squirt! A fine mist landed on Gordon's back. He threw back his head and brayed.

"He doesn't like it!" Annie gasped, dropping her brush in surprise. As she knelt to pick it up, Gordon did one of his neat little butts. Annie sprawled forward into the straw.

"Oops!" Eva giggled. "Are you OK?"

Frowning, Annie stood up. "Are you sure this goat's safe?" she asked.

"Yeah, look." Confidently Eva stepped up to Gordon and began to brush his long, smooth coat.

Gordon flinched and lowered his head.

"Watch out!" Annie warned.

The goat had his eye on the stable door. He stamped his feet and snorted. Then, with one sudden, mad dash he charged.

"The door – I didn't bolt it!" Annie cried.

Eva threw herself headlong at the door, but it was too late. Gordon reached it first, barged through and fled from the stables.

"Oh no!" Eva gasped. Picking herself up, she ran after him.

Gordon was fast. He raced across the yard, up on to the dung heap and over the fence into Guinevere and Merlin's field.

"Oh – oh!" a desperate Annie cried, chasing after Eva. "Mum will kill us if he scares the horses!"

By this time, Karl had come running and Linda Brooks had flung open her back door. Hearing the commotion, a puzzled Heidi and Mark emerged from the house.

"Gordon escaped!" Annie shouted. "Eva's gone after him!"

"Oh, great!" Karl muttered. "The Wesleys are on their way to see him right this minute."

"Eva, wait! Take a head collar!" Mark yelled.

But Eva was already vaulting over the fence in hot pursuit of the goat. Gordon was charging across the lush green field, kicking up his heels and making a terrible racket.

"Get that horrid thing out of my field!" Linda wailed as she stood by her fence.

"Uh-oh!" Heidi sighed. Just when they thought they'd got Linda Brooks on their side at last, something like this had to happen. "Now Linda will be up in arms against Animal Magic all over again."

"Never mind, I expect the council have already decided whether or not to keep us open," Mark assured her. "We're waiting for a letter in the post any day, remember."

"Yes, but..." Heidi muttered, shaking her head.

Meanwhile, Eva chased Gordon up and down the field. "Come back!" she called, waving her arms and skirting round the back of Guinevere and Merlin.

Guinevere whisked her long, white tail and laid back her ears. Little Merlin stuck close to his mother's side.

Gordon cantered on, kicking up his heels and enjoying his freedom. He felt the breeze on his face and the sunshine on his back – no way was he planning to surrender.

"Come here!" Eva yelled again as Gordon doubled back and galloped up the hill.

Karl stood astride the fence watching. "She's never going to catch him," he told his dad.

"Annie, how did that creature get into my field?" Linda Brooks demanded as soon as she spotted her daughter in the yard next door.

"It was my fault," Annie confessed. "I didn't bolt his door."

Karl shrugged, turning just in time to see a red car enter the yard. He groaned as he saw two strangers climb out.

"Stop him!" Linda cried as Gordon sprinted straight towards her fence. She cowered against an apple tree and closed her eyes in fright.

"...Mr and Mrs Wesley!" Karl said, faking a smile at the strangers.

A small, middle-aged man in a grey sweatshirt and jeans and a taller woman wearing jodhpurs and stable boots stared at the chaos.

"We came to see the goat," Mr Wesley

began, "but perhaps it isn't a good time?"

Just at that moment, galloping Gordon made a great leap over Linda Brooks's fence into her garden. He'd spotted marigolds and mallows, and better still – lettuces and peas growing in neat rows. Fabulous fodder!

"Help!" Linda cried from under the apple tree. "Shoo, you horrible thing! Leave my lettuces alone!"

"Gordon, come back!" Eva cried, staggering breathlessly up the hill.

The goat munched and trampled, munched again.

"Is that him?" Mrs Wesley stepped up to the fence and peered with horror into Linda's wrecked garden.

Gordon glanced up. He had a mouthful of crunchy young lettuce and a wicked look in his eye.

"That's him," Karl groaned, as Mr and Mrs Wesley shook their heads.

"Oh dear!" Mr Wesley turned to his wife. "Gordon seems to be more of a handful than we've been led to expect."

"Yes," Mrs Wesley agreed. "We'd better go home and have a good talk about it."

"Terrific!" Karl groaned, as he watched Gordon's potential owners walk swiftly away.

Chapter Five

"You win some, you lose some," Mark told Karl as the Wesleys' red car drove slowly out of the yard. "There's never any guarantee that things will work out as planned."

But Karl was furious. "How come you're not telling Eva off?" he wanted to know. "If she and Annie hadn't been messing about in Gordon's stable, this would never have happened."

Annie cringed, then crept quietly away.

"We weren't 'messing about'. We were grooming him!" Eva yelled from next-door's garden. Red faced and breathless, she was still trying to corner the runaway.

"Try this." Heidi passed Gordon's bucket of cabbage leaves over the fence, together with a head collar and lead rope from the stables.

Eva held out the tempting food. "Lovely, yummy cabbage!" she cooed.

Gordon raised his head and flared his nostrils. He edged close to the bucket, his top lip quivering. As he stretched his neck to grab a bite, Eva swiftly slung the rope around his neck.

"Good job," Heidi said, as Gordon let out a loud, surprised bray.

"Get him out of here!" Linda screeched. "Just look at the mess. He's ruined my lettuce patch!"

Tugging with all her strength, Eva managed to lead Gordon up Linda's drive.

"Gosh, you're stubborn," she muttered, steering him next door.

Gordon's hooves clattered across the yard towards his stable.

"Watch out, don't get behind him," Mark said. "He'll kick you given half a chance."

Huffing and puffing, Eva finally got the Houdini goat back into his stall.

"What now?" Karl demanded. "The Wesleys will never adopt Gordon after what they've just seen."

"Sorry!" Eva gasped. "That wasn't meant to happen."

"OK, let's all calm down," Heidi said. "I'm sure there'll be other possible owners. If you ask me, our main problem right now is not finding a home for Gordon, it's Linda and her lettuces."

"Don't worry, I'll go and smooth things over," Mark volunteered.

"And I'll get back on the website and start all over again," Karl muttered, going off with a deep frown.

In the quiet aftermath Heidi looked at Eva. "Are you OK?"

Eva sniffed and nodded.

"Fed up?"

She nodded again.

Heidi smiled and gave Eva's hand a squeeze. "Come on, let's go and check on Rusty. It's time to give him another feed."

"His temperature's still high but his pulse is regular," Joel reported as Eva sat down with the fox cub on her lap.

Heidi handed her the syringe. "Don't worry, the effect of the antibiotics will soon kick in," she promised. "Try and get as much of this milk down him as you can. It'll keep his strength up."

Eva nodded, then gently opened the cub's mouth. He stared up at her with his golden brown eyes as she slid the tip of the syringe into his mouth. "There!" she murmured. "It tastes good, doesn't it?"

Rusty gulped then swallowed.

"Good boy. Are you nice and warm in your bed?" Eva talked softly as Rusty fed, taking care not to touch his injured foot. "He's drinking well," she told her mum.

"It looks as if he could be on the mend." Heidi gave a satisfied nod then went to take a look at the five kittens in the nearby bay. "Have you given these kittens names yet?" she asked Eva.

"Rosa, Tulip, Stella, Timmy and Ringo." Eva ran through the names. "Karl's already put them on the website." She gave Rusty the last drops of milk, then cuddled him close.

Her mum glanced at her over her shoulder. She turned with a small frown. "Try not to cuddle and pet Rusty too much, Eva."

Eva frowned back. "Why not? He loves it – see!"

As if to prove her point, the tiny cub licked Eva's cheek.

"Exactly," Heidi said in a professional tone. "But it's important not to handle him too much. He's not the same as a kitten or a puppy."

"Yes he is. You're just as fluffy and cute, aren't you, Rusty?" Smiling, Eva tickled the cub on the white flash under his chin.

"Eva, you're not listening. What I'm saying is, he's not a pet." Heidi came over and took the cub from her.

Rusty let out a tiny, sharp bark.

"Watch out for his poorly leg!" Eva cried.

"I am watching out." Heidi put Rusty back in his unit. "We have to handle him as little as possible. If he gets too used to us, he won't want to go back into the wild."

"Go back?" Eva echoed, surprised.

"Yes. When — if — he gets better. We'll put him back where you found him and hope that he finds his family again."

"Oh!" Eva hadn't thought that far ahead. Put him back by the dark, dangerous river, in the long grass amongst those shadowy thorn bushes?

"Yes. Rusty's a wild animal. He belongs in the woods and along the river bank. I thought you realized that?"

Eva nodded quickly. "Course I did," she insisted, trying to sound sensible. "I knew all along we'd have to put him back."

"So don't make a pet of him. And don't get too attached," Heidi warned as she left the cattery.

Tears welled up in Eva's eyes as she gazed at the fox cub curled up on his blanket. He blinked and licked his lips to taste the last drops of milk.

"Too late!" Eva murmured, brushing away a tear. "I fell in love with you the moment I first saw you!"

Chapter Six

"Why can't you keep him?" Annie asked Eva.

It was Sunday morning in the yard at Animal Magic, and the two girls had brought Guinevere and Merlin in from the field. Despite a fine drizzle, they had decided to ride.

"Stand still while I tighten your girth," Eva told Guinevere. She'd just told Annie what her mum had said about Rusty.

"Why?" Annie asked again.

"Because he's a wild animal," Eva muttered.

"But lots of people keep wild animals as pets," Annie pointed out, putting on her hard hat. "I read in the newspaper about a woman who adopted a lion cub and led him about on a dog lead!"

"Hmm." Eva frowned. "I don't know..." She'd lain awake half the night, worrying about Rusty going back to the wild and imagining what it would be like to keep him. *I could house-train him and take him for walks*, she thought. *He would come to me when I called his name!*

"It would be so cool to give Rusty a home!" Annie sighed. She stroked Guinevere's nose then put her foot in the stirrup. "That's what Animal Magic is all about, isn't it?"

Eva ignored the question and held the

reins while Annie mounted. "About that lion cub on a lead… What happens when the cub gets too big to be taken for walks?"

"Yeah, I know," Annie agreed. "But that wouldn't happen with Rusty, would it? He'll never grow that big."

"Don't go on about it," Eva pleaded. "It's bad enough already."

Glancing down at her friend, Annie saw how miserable she was. "I'm sure your mum knows what she's talking about. There's probably a law against it or something," she sighed. "Only, y'know, people do feed foxes and they get quite tame. I read about it in—"

"Annie!" Eva groaned.

"OK, sorry." Pressing her heels against Guinevere's sides, Annie set off across the yard. She waited at the gates while Eva fetched her bike from the shed. "Anyway, how is Rusty this morning? Is he getting better?"

Wobbling past Annie and Guinevere on her bike, Eva led the way along the quiet, damp village street. "Joel says he had a good night," she reported. "When I saw him this morning, his eyes were bright. He was more lively. In fact, yeah, I think he's slowly getting better, fingers crossed!"

"Did you see Linda this morning?" Mark asked Eva over Sunday dinner. He was tucking in to a mountain of roast potatoes.

"No, why?" She and Annie had ridden

for an hour, taking it in turns. They'd crossed the river on the road bridge and hacked out through the woods beyond the golf course.

"I just wondered what sort of mood she's in," her dad mumbled. "Whoo, these potatoes are hot!"

"She's in a mega-foul mood," Karl reported. "She nabbed me just as I was crossing the yard. She wanted to know when you're going to plant some new lettuces."

"As soon as I've had the chance to ask Dad to drop some off from the garden centre," Mark explained. "Until then, we'd better all wear hard hats when we go out, and beware sniper fire from next door!"

"Uh!" Heidi grunted, shaking her head. "Yesterday's little episode with Gordon is the last thing we needed."

"It wasn't Gordon's fault," Karl reminded them as he glared across the table at Eva. "By the way, I got an email from the Wesleys this morning, confirming that they didn't think he was the goat for them!"

"Never mind." As usual, Heidi refused to be downhearted. "I saw two couples this morning who want to adopt kittens. So Tulip and Ringo are all set up with nice new homes."

"And Rusty is getting stronger all the time," Mark added. "At this rate, we should be able to set him free by the end of next week."

Eva put down her knife and fork and pushed her plate away.

"Not hungry?" her mum asked quietly.

Eva shook her head. "Can I go and help Joel, please?"

Heidi nodded. "That would be good. Tell him to take his lunch break while you're over there keeping an eye on things."

Eva slipped out of the house and made her way across the yard. She went into the kennels and then into the cattery, looking for Joel who was nowhere to be seen. Back on the porch outside Reception, the noise of a door being bolted inside the stable block told Eva that Joel was visiting Gordon.

Eva set off towards the stables then

quickly changed her mind. She retraced her steps into the cattery, saying hi to Rosa and the rest of the litter, then stopping close to the fox cub's unit. "Hi, Rusty," she murmured, longing to pick him up and cuddle him.

No! she told herself. *Don't pet him!*

Rusty looked up at her with bright eyes. He uncurled himself and stretched. Then he stood gingerly, taking care not to put weight on his injured leg.

"You're beautiful!" Eva breathed. "And so little!"

She gazed at the tiny fox cub's shiny, rust-brown coat with the clean white flash on his chest. His pointed ears were pricked, his amber eyes shone. With his sore foot raised, Rusty tilted his head and gazed back at her.

"So little!" she repeated. Much too small

to be set free and made to fend for himself amongst the long grass and thorn bushes, beside the dangerous water of the fast-flowing river.

"And so helpless," she whispered fearfully. "Oh Rusty, I can't bear it. Why do you have to go?"

Chapter Seven

"Has the post arrived?" Karl asked when he appeared at breakfast the next morning.

"Nope." Eva had been up for hours. Even though the summer holidays had begun, she didn't have lie-ins – not when there were dogs to walk, kittens to feed, Rusty to look after ... the list was endless.

Karl went to the front door to check the mat, just in case.

"He's worried about the letter from the

council," Heidi guessed. She'd popped into the house for a coffee after a busy session of canine dentistry. "Jasper's teeth are much better," she told them. "And I've given all the dogs their wormers. When I go back across, I plan to microchip Rosa's litter."

"Can I feed Rusty?" Eva asked. She knew it was Joel's day off and jumped at the chance to step in.

"Yes, please." Swallowing the last of her coffee, Heidi rushed on ahead.

"You only offered 'cos you want a chance to cuddle him," Karl scoffed.

"So?" Eva blushed.

"So, he should be learning to feed from a saucer by now, ready for F Day."

"Ready for what?"

"F Day. Freedom Day, in case you'd forgotten."

Eva's heart sank. "Shut up, Karl," she muttered as she dashed after her mum.

"Hey, Rusty!" Eva murmured. She settled the fox cub on her lap.

Rusty looked around eagerly for his milk, twitching his ears and flicking his little tail.

"Yes, you know what's coming, don't you? Here you are!"

As Eva slid the dropper between his lips, the cub gulped greedily. Soon all the milk was gone.

"Good boy!" Eva smiled. She tickled him under his chin then let him lick her fingers. "You're doing really well, you know that?"

Rusty's temperature was back to normal. His leg was healing rapidly. For a tiny second Eva gave way to the temptation to hug him.

"Good news!" Karl burst into the cattery. "I checked the emails and we've got another enquiry about Gordon!" He broke off as he spotted Eva with Rusty.

Guiltily she put him back in the unit.

"I saw that!" Karl cried. "You know you're not supposed to pet that cub!"

"I wasn't ... I didn't ..." Eva shook her head. "Give me a break, Karl!"

But her brother was still angry with her over Gordon. "You know what Mum said – Rusty will never survive in the wild if you handle him all the time."

"It's not all the time. I just picked him up to feed him."

"Yeah well, it'll be your fault if he doesn't survive out there." With this, Karl barged out of the door.

Eva's heart thumped. She swallowed hard as she gazed down at Rusty. "I'm sorry ... I didn't mean ... I mean ... oh dear!"

The cub gave her a bright stare. He cocked his head to one side and sat back on his hind legs, for all the world like a puppy inviting her to play.

"Oh!" Eva panicked. "What if Karl's right? What if I have wrecked your chances of making it out in the wild?"

Though it was one of the hardest things Eva had ever had to do, she kept away from Rusty all through Monday and Tuesday. By Wednesday evening, Heidi reported that the cub had fought off the infection and was now eating small amounts of kitten food from a saucer.

"Terrific," Mark said. "When do his stitches come out?"

"Friday," Heidi said. "By the way, when are you going to plant those new lettuces for Linda? She was nagging me about them earlier today."

"As it happens..." Mark began.

They watched him go outside to his van and return with a box of lettuce seedlings.

"I called in at the garden centre on the way home from work," he explained. "Eva, do you want to come next door and help me plant them?"

Eva nodded, keen to keep busy and not worry about Rusty.

Her dad grinned. "Great! You can protect me from the dreaded Linda. Come on!"

"So what's wrong?" Mark asked as he and Eva knelt side by side in Linda's vegetable patch.

Only Jason was in, but he'd told Mark and Eva to go ahead with the planting.

"Nothing's wrong," Eva fibbed.

"So why are you so quiet? It's not like you." Dropping a seedling into a small hole, Mark firmed up the soil around it.

"No reason. I'm fine."

"Have you had an argument with Karl?"

"No. Well yeah."

"About Gordon? Is that little feud still bubbling away?"

Eva copied her dad and planted another seedling. "Kind of."

They worked for a while in silence, making sure that their rows of seedlings were straight. "Karl can be a bit of a know-all sometimes," her dad began again. "Y'know, like most big brothers. But don't let him get to you."

"I don't," Eva protested, glad for once to see Linda's car driving through the gates.

Annie jumped out and hurried over. "Hi, Eva! Do you fancy taking Guinevere out? You can ride first if you want."

"No time now. Maybe tomorrow," Eva said, cringing as Annie's mum approached.

Mark looked up from his planting. "These are the best Webbs lettuces," he told Linda. "Hand picked and donated by my dad."

Linda inspected the newly planted rows.

"Well?" Mark asked.

"Not bad," Linda acknowledged slowly. "You've planted them nice and straight. You and Eva have done a good job."

"Thank you, m'lady!" Mark stood up, tugging his forelock and grinning. "So are we quits?"

Linda sniffed and held her head high. But gradually her face softened into a smile. "Yes, you and Gordon are officially forgiven! In fact, why don't you and Eva come inside for a cup of tea?"

"Relief!" Mark sighed. "You hear that, Eva and Annie? You're both witnesses!"

"Don't push it, Mark," Linda warned. "And don't let that goat near my garden ever again!"

"Linda actually said she was sorry for getting up the petition in the first place," Mark told Heidi when he and Eva went to look for her in the cattery.

Heidi had just admitted a feral cat brought in from an allotment on the edge of Okeham village. The poor creature was thin and scraggy, with a mass of tangled grey fur.

"Sorry is not a word I ever expected to hear from Linda's lips," Heidi admitted.

"I know. She was talking about it over a cup of tea after we'd finished planting the lettuces. I almost fell off my chair."

As her parents chatted, Eva sneaked a look at Rusty.

As soon as the fox cub spotted her, he tried to clamber up the side of his unit.

"No. Stay down, Rusty. I'm not allowed to pick you up," she murmured.

"Linda's sorry she's caused us all this worry about being closed down," Mark went on. "And now she admits she'd never have had the chance to adopt Guinevere and Merlin if it hadn't been for Animal Magic."

"Wow," Heidi said, then tutted. "Better late than never, I guess."

"...Stay down, Rusty," Eva insisted.

"You resisted him – well done!" her mum said. "Rusty's way too cute for his own good."

"Totally," Eva sighed, shaking her head as she tore herself away.

Her dad stared quietly after her. "Aha," he told Heidi softly. "Now I know what's got into Eva!"

Chapter Eight

"What's really bothering you?" Eva's dad asked her.

For once, the whole family had got together the next evening to relax in front of the telly. It was Thursday, and Karl and Heidi wanted to watch a wildlife programme that followed the migration of three wild swans across the frozen wastes of the Canadian Rockies.

"Everything!" Eva admitted.

Her dad cosied up next to her on the

sofa and put an arm around her shoulder. "It's Rusty, isn't it?" he said quietly. "That's what's making you miserable."

Eva sighed and nodded.

"Tell me more," Mark invited gently.

"Sshh!" Karl said, as he turned up the volume on the television.

"We won't know how he's getting on after we set him free," Eva answered. "He'll be all alone. And it's scary out there, especially at night."

Her dad nodded thoughtfully. "I understand how you feel, but I'm afraid that's life. It's something you're going to have to accept."

"But cars speed down these lanes, Dad. Rusty might be crossing the road and...' Eva tailed off. "...And even if he doesn't get squished, what will he eat? What if he starves? And what if he has to be alone for the rest of his life?"

"I don't know. But as far as I can see, there's nothing we can do to keep track of a wild animal once we release it."

"So how do they track these swans?" Heidi showed that she'd been half listening to their conversation as she watched the telly. "Karl, do you know how they know which bird is which?"

Eva and Mark switched their attention to the screen. They watched a large flock of swans sailing on air currents over snow-covered mountains.

"Easy. It told you at the start of the programme – they fix tiny radio transmitters to their legs," Karl explained. "You set a special signal for each bird. The film-makers receive the signal on a really cool receiver, like a mobile phone."

"Clever stuff," Mark said.

Eva stared at the wild birds soaring through the blue sky. "Wow!" she said. "That means they can track them wherever they go!"

"Whoa, just a minute!" Mark warned, worried that Eva was about to come up with one of her brilliant ideas.

"No, that's really interesting," Heidi interrupted. "I was at college with a woman called Su Jones who tracked a male badger for six months with a tiny transmitter fixed to the base of his ear. It was her special project."

"But, hang on." Mark glanced at Eva. It was too late. Her eyes were gleaming. She was taking in every word.

"We could do that with Rusty!" Eva gasped. "We could get a tiny radio and fix it to his ear. Then we'd know exactly where he was!"

"Yeah, but where do we find one of those?" Mark asked. "Don't you need an expert to fit it? Aren't they very expensive?"

"Mum can ask her friend, Su!" Eva exclaimed. She sprang up from the sofa. "Where does Su live now?"

"Not far. About twenty miles away. I'm still in touch with her from time to time." Heidi gave the idea serious thought. "You know, it might be worth giving her a call."

"Now!" Eva insisted. Suddenly her

whole world had turned on its head. If swans flew over massive mountain ranges giving off radio signals, why couldn't a little fox cub go beep-beep as he roamed through the undergrowth at the bottom of Linda's field?

Heidi raised her eyebrows as she glanced at Mark. Karl had his face glued to the television as usual. "It's worth a try," she decided.

"Now, Mum!" Eva said again, dragging Heidi towards the phone. As they left

the room, she fell on Karl and gave him a hug.

He shrank back. "Yuck. What was that for?"

"For giving us a totally cool idea!" Eva cried, and danced out of the room.

"Joel, could you bring the light closer to the table?" It was Friday morning. Heidi, Joel and Eva were gathered around the surgery table. Eva had sprayed the surface and wiped it clean before her mum had arrived with Rusty.

"That's better. Now we can see exactly what we're doing," Heidi said as she pulled on a pair of blue surgical gloves. "Eva, keep a tight hold of Rusty while I quickly take out his stitches."

Gently, Eva held the cub still. He sat quietly, curling his pink tongue across his top lip, his eyes darting this way and that.

"Perfect," Heidi announced after the job was done. "Now hang on to him while I pierce his ear and put in this sterile pin."

"Your friend, Su, told you how this thing

works?" Joel asked, watching with interest.

Heidi nodded. "I went over to see her early this morning. She was glad to give us the device and explain the whole thing. This pin has a small tag which glows in the dark and sends off a radio signal. The receiver is that thing that looks like a mobile phone lying on the shelf over there. We set it to the right frequency and it picks up Rusty's whereabouts from a distance of five kilometres. The signal gets louder as you get closer to the transmitter, and vice versa."

Joel picked up the receiver and turned it over, examining it closely.

Swiftly, Heidi pierced the cub's ear, almost without him seeming to notice. The tag was firmly in place.

"See, that didn't hurt," Eva whispered.

"OK, back into the unit!" Heidi ordered.

Eva whisked the cub from the table and carried him back into the cattery.

"Hey, Dusty!" she sang out to the stray allotment cat who was now on the Animal Magic website. She placed Rusty in his unit. "Until tonight!" she murmured.

Tonight was the big night – Freedom Night.

And now Eva wasn't so afraid for little Rusty. OK, so it was still a big, scary world out there, and yes, maybe Eva had made him too much of a pet, but when you looked at him, how could you resist?

At least, now, with this little pin in his ear, they would know exactly where he was and that he was safe!

"See you later, Rusty," Eva whispered.

She closed the door of the cattery with her fingers crossed, half-afraid, half-excited about what lay ahead.

Chapter Nine

"Don't go near Gordon!" Karl warned as Eva went out into the yard.

She'd left Joel and her mum to work out exactly how the radio receiver worked and had bumped into Karl.

"Why not?" Eva wanted to know.

"A man called Eric is on his way to see him right now. And you know what happened last time with the Wesleys."

"OK, OK, no need to rub it in!" Eva laughed. No way was grumpy Karl going to spoil Rusty's special day.

"Just don't go near him with sprays and brushes, OK!" Karl grumbled.

"Oh please, let me de-tangle him and make him pretty!" she said wickedly, advancing towards the stables.

Karl blocked Eva's way. "Very funny!" he muttered as a muddy Land Rover turned into the yard.

Out stepped an old man in a worn tweed jacket and wellington boots. He was bald and stooping; his face was wrinkled.

"Hello, er – Eric?" Karl said uncertainly.

"Where's this goat of yours?" The visitor got straight down to business, marching into the stable and taking a long, hard look at Gordon.

"Scary man!" Eva mouthed at Karl behind the visitor's back. She saw a black and white Border collie sitting patiently in the Land Rover.

"Yeah," Karl whispered back.

They followed him inside.

Boldly, Eric went up to Gordon and ran a hand through his silky coat. Then to Gordon's surprise, the old man slid his fingers into the goat's mouth and checked his teeth.

"Hmm," Eric said.

Gordon snickered uneasily as the visitor firmly closed his mouth then picked up one foot at a time to inspect his hooves.

"Good boy, Gordon!" Karl muttered nervously. Any second now, the goat was going to floor the old man with a mighty kick.

"Nice pedigree," Eric reported. "Good condition. Well done, lad."

"Well done, who? Me or Gordon?" Karl whispered to Eva.

She shrugged. Didn't Eric know the risk he was taking if he pushed Gordon around like that?

But Gordon stood meekly having his feet lifted and his mouth inspected a second time.

"The thing is, I don't know if I really need a billy goat right now," the old man explained as he emerged unscathed from Gordon's stall.

Gordon stood with a puzzled expression. Eva thought he was probably wondering why he hadn't managed to get in a quick headbutt.

"I run a small herd of goats at a farm over the other side of the valley," Eric told Eva and Karl. "My son spotted this one on your website and said I should come and take a look."

"A goat farm?" Karl checked out the visitor. Now the muddy Land Rover and the patient dog made sense. "Hey, Gordon, doesn't that sound cool?"

Eric frowned and jutted out his bottom lip. "Listen, I'm not saying for certain that I'll take him off your hands. I only came to give him a quick glance."

Karl and Eva nodded and exchanged hopeful looks. They'd definitely got over their first impression of Eric as Mr Scary.

"As I say, I don't really need a billy goat. The one I have, Tyson, is a handful as it is."

Eva thought fast. "Yes, but Gordon isn't hard to handle," she pointed out, as if butter wouldn't melt in her mouth. "You saw for yourself, he's really gentle!"

Karl's eyes almost popped out of his head at this, but he didn't say a word.

"And like you said, he's in lovely condition," Eva added.

In the background, Gordon let out a bray to tell them that he knew they were talking about him.

Eric nodded and strode back to his Land Rover. "Let me think about it and have a word with my son, Josh," he told them as he sat behind the wheel.

"I'll be in touch," he said, starting the engine and pulling out of the yard.

"Will he or won't he?" Eva asked. She'd done her best to convince Eric to give Gordon what sounded like a fab new home.

Karl shrugged. "Fingers crossed," he muttered.

"They're already crossed," Eva replied, holding up both hands. "For Rusty and now for Gordon. Let's hope that everything works out OK!"

That evening, Eva and Heidi went alone to the place on the river bank where Eva had found Rusty exactly a week earlier.

Eva carried him across the field in a lightweight pet carrier, following the beam of her mum's torch. "Mum, did you bring the radio receiver?" she double-checked.

"In my jacket pocket," Heidi replied, as they reached the fence. "Here, let me hold Rusty while you climb over."

"Did you test the battery?" Eva asked.

"Yes."

"What about the transmitter? Are you sure it's working?"

Following Eva over the fence, Heidi landed on the sloping river bank. The torchlight wobbled and wavered across the dark, rapid water. "No more questions, Eva. Everything's in order. Let's just do it!"

Eva took a deep breath and placed the carrier carefully on the ground. She crouched beside it and opened the door. Inside, Rusty sat with his pointed ears pricked, his fiery eyes glinting in the torch beam.

"Come out, Rusty, it's time to go," she whispered.

But the fox cub seemed to be in no hurry. He lifted one paw and licked it, then the other.

"He doesn't want to leave. Shall I lift him out?" Eva asked.

"No. Let him find his own way. Wait a sec while I kill the light and turn on the receiver."

At the press of a button on the small handset, a clear beeping sound broke the night's silence.

Inside the carrier, Rusty pricked his ears then crept forward until he teetered at the edge. As he picked up scents in the grass, he ducked his head and sniffed hard.

"Good boy!" Heidi encouraged.

"Look, the little tag does glow in the dark!" Eva breathed, watching the small green light attached to Rusty's ear.

Growing braver, the cub ventured out into the long grass. He seemed alert, listening to every swish and crackle of his surroundings.

Beep-beep went the signal as Rusty took his first steps back into nature.

"So far, so good," Heidi murmured.

Eva crouched quietly, watching Rusty dig at the soft earth with one of his front paws. He sniffed again, then trotted on a few steps.

Come back! her heart said. But her head knew he must go.

Beep-beep. The signal sounded loud and clear.

Rusty trotted on along the river bank, half hidden by the thorn bushes. Then he stopped and turned to look straight at Eva. He paused and tilted his head to one side.

It's like he's asking me a question, Eva thought, her heart beating fast. *Is it OK if I go now?*

"He's saying thank you and goodbye," Heidi whispered.

"Goodbye, Rusty!" Eva murmured, her heart racing. He looked calm and happy out here, ready to carry on with his old life in the wild.

The fox cub swished his tail. His eyes glinted. Then he turned and disappeared down the slope.

Chapter Ten

Eva slept badly that night, tossing and turning and rerunning in her mind the moment when Rusty had turned his head to say goodbye. A magical, sad moment in the moonlight.

She got up early to turn on the radio receiver and listen.

Beep-beep-beep. Rusty's signal came through loud and clear.

Sighing, Eva went into the cattery. Animal Magic seemed empty without

Rusty, but Dusty the allotment cat was miaowing loudly, so Eva gave her a saucer of fresh milk.

"Eva, are you there?" Annie's faint voice floated through from Reception.

"Coming!" she replied, going to greet her friend.

"How did it go last night?" Annie asked.

"Good. Rusty trotted off along the river bank, no problem."

"Did he look scared?"

"No. Pretty confident, actually."

"And are you getting a signal?" Annie pestered. She wanted to hear every detail about the fox cub's release.

Eva took out the receiver and turned it on. "Listen!"

Beep-beep-beep.

Annie grinned. "How cool is that! But sad as well."

Eva nodded. "I miss him," she confessed.

"I know. But Eva, guess what. Mum called Mr Winters at the Council again, saying she definitely wanted to withdraw the petition against Animal Magic!"

Eva sat down on a stool with a loud gasp.

"I know. I couldn't believe it either."

"How come she's done it again?" Eva asked.

"It's Guinevere and Merlin," Annie explained. "Ever since we adopted them, she's been feeling worse and worse about wanting to have you closed down. She kept talking to Dad about it and in the end she rang again."

"So did they say we can stay open?"

"Ah!" Annie cleared her throat. "Not exactly. It turns out that Mr Winters reminded Mum it wasn't as simple as that."

"Ah," Eva echoed, but more quietly.

"He said a lot of other people had signed the petition. And anyway, it wasn't up to him."

"So who is it up to?"

"The whole Council. And they've already decided," Annie told her.

"So?" As quickly as Eva's hopes rose, they fell again.

"Mr Winters wouldn't tell Mum over the phone. But he said the letter to your mum and dad was definitely in the post."

"Well, it didn't come this morning," Eva muttered. "And it's Sunday tomorrow."

"So it'll arrive on Monday." Annie held up her hand with her fingers crossed. "Here's hoping that it's a yes for Animal Magic."

"I don't have enough fingers," Eva sighed. "Come on, let's go and walk Jasper."

Chapter Eleven

Walk the dogs, feed the cats, muck out Gordon's stall. The list of Saturday jobs went on and on.

"Take a break, Eva," her mum insisted. It was early evening and Eva was flopped on a chair in Reception, looking tired. "Go over to the house and grab a sandwich."

"Can I take the receiver with me?" All day Eva had kept it by her side, reassured by the faint beep-beep of Rusty's signal.

Heidi nodded and smiled. "Rusty's

doing OK, believe me!"

"I still want to listen," Eva insisted. She trudged across the yard, kicked off her boots in the kitchen doorway and went inside.

"You didn't go near Gordon, did you?" Karl asked suspiciously. He too was re-fuelling with a giant cheese sandwich.

"I had to muck him out," Eva retorted, washing her hands before she cut into the loaf.

"Did you bolt his door properly?"

"Yeah, yeah. Anyway, did Eric call back?"

"Not yet." Casually Karl picked up the radio handset. As he fiddled with the volume, the beeping sound gradually faded then died.

"Hey, what happened?" Eva took the receiver from him. "What did you do?"

"Nothing. It just stopped. Give it back.

Let me try again."

"We lost the signal!" Eva wailed. She felt panic rise inside her.

Karl tapped buttons without success. "Yeah, we lost it," he agreed at last.

"Karl, you don't think...?" Eva couldn't put into words a dreadful idea that had come into her head.

"What? That something bad has happened to Rusty?" Karl frowned. He remembered the wild swans flying over the mountains. One of them had stopped transmitting, and then they'd found him ... out of range, and dead!

Eva could hardly breathe. "We've got to do something! Try again, Karl. The transmitter can't fall off, can it?"

"No way. Look, I think we should go and look for Rusty."

"Yes!" Eva agreed. "Right now. Come on,

Karl. Bring the transmitter!" Slipping her boots back on, she ran outside and headed for the river.

Rusty could have drowned! He could have been run over, chased, even killed!

Eva's imagination ran riot as she and Karl sprinted across Guinevere's field.

"Still no signal," Karl reported as they reached the spot on the river bank where Eva and Heidi had released the cub into the wild.

Eva knelt down in the long grass. She felt like crying, but she forced herself to carry on searching.

"Which way did he go?" Karl asked.

"Towards the bridge." Eva pointed out the direction. "We're never going to find his tracks, though. He's too small and light."

"Let's try," Karl insisted. He stepped carefully along the bank, looking out for tiny footprints in the soft mud.

"It's hopeless," Eva sighed as they reached the bridge. Still the receiver was silent. There was no sign of life from Rusty.

"We keep on trying," Karl insisted. "Maybe Rusty went out of range – y'know, too far away for the receiver to pick up his signal."

"He can't have. He's too little to travel

five kilometres in one day."

"You're probably right. And the signal did get cut off suddenly. It didn't fade and then stop."

"So which way now?" Eva asked miserably.

"Over the bridge," Karl decided.

With fading hope, Eva and Karl crossed the old stone bridge.

"Left or right?" Karl asked.

Eva looked to the right, at the golf course with its smooth, open greens. To the left was the small wood. If Rusty had any sense, he would seek shelter there. "Left," she decided.

On they went in the failing light, into the shadow of the tall trees. Step by step Eva grew more certain that something terrible had happened to Rusty.

"This is all my fault," she moaned. "If I

hadn't petted him and made him tame, he would have stood a better chance."

"Shut up, Eva!" Karl said gruffly. Then he spoke more kindly. "Forget what I said earlier. This isn't down to you. Out here in the wild, it's just luck whether or not a fox cub makes it."

Eva sniffed, then listened to the sounds all around, peering between the wide trunks of two horse chestnuts. "What was that? I thought I saw something move."

"It's nothing," Karl decided, staring at the handset and turning the volume to maximum. "But hang on a minute, I think we're picking up a signal again!"

Beep-beep, beep-beep.

"Yes!" Eva gasped. "It's faint, but it's there!"

"This way!" Karl said, setting off in the direction where the signal grew louder.

Not dead. Not attacked and killed. Still alive... Please!

Now each step took them closer to Rusty. The signal strengthened as they sprinted between trees, over logs and through thick bushes.

"Shh!" Karl warned. In the gloom of the woods, they'd picked up the loudest signal yet. "Let's stop and keep watch!"

Eva and Karl crouched down behind the mossy trunk of a fallen tree.

Beep-beep-beep. The signal didn't weaken, but grew stronger.

Shadows seemed to move as their eyes played tricks. "Look!" Eva leaped up, convinced that she'd seen a small animal hiding behind a tree trunk.

"Squirrel!" Karl whispered, pulling her back down.

Beep-beep. The signal of hope.

Then at last it happened. A shape appeared out of a hole in the earth. Amber eyes glinted.

"Oh!" Eva sighed. This time she stayed hidden behind the tree trunk.

A grown fox came into view. They could just make her out – her pointed ears, sleek body and magnificent, furry tail. She looked this way and that, sniffed the air and waited.

Then a baby fox tumbled out of the half-hidden hole, and another. Two cubs following their mother.

"Which one is Rusty?" Karl whispered.

"Neither," Eva answered. She was waiting for a cub with a pierced ear and a transmitter glowing with a dim green light.

And here it was! A third baby emerged from the hole, skipping quickly after the other two, shaking himself and yawning.

Beep-beep-beep. The signal sounded louder than ever.

"Rusty found his family!" Eva sighed.

"Or they found him," Karl added.

"Whichever." Eva didn't care. All that mattered was that Rusty was alive and well ... and back where he belonged!

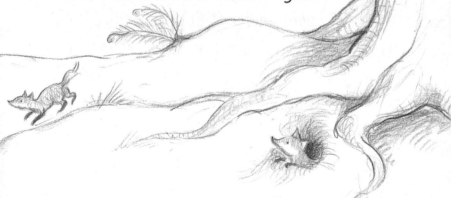

"The mystery is solved!" Heidi smiled broadly as the family sat down to a meal late that night. "You lost the signal because Rusty was in his den!"

"And the transmitter doesn't work underground," Mark explained to Karl and Eva. "We'll have to remember that in future."

"But we saw him!" Eva cried. "He's got brothers and sisters. He's got a mum again!"

"Brilliant," her dad said.

"And it was like nothing bad had ever happened." Still bubbling with excitement, Eva ignored her food. "His mum watched over him and kept him in line."

"As mums do," Mark grinned, when Heidi told Eva to finish her supper.

"We watched them for about ten minutes," Karl reported. "Then they trotted off between the trees. You could still see them in the moonlight."

"So gorgeous!" Eva sighed.

"So sometimes what we do here at Animal Magic is not about rehoming," Heidi pointed out.

"Sometimes it's about freedom." Mark finished her thought.

"Talking of rehoming," Eva and Karl's dad remembered. "Eric Greene called when you were out. He says he's talked things over with his son and they'll be glad to take Gordon off our hands. They can pick him up tomorrow."

Eva and Karl jumped up from the table and gave a high five.

"Cool!" Karl said.

"A new home!" Eva cried.

"Where are you going?" her mum protested as Eva headed for the door.

"To talk to Gordon!" she insisted, sprinting across the yard and flinging open the stable door.

Laughing, Mark and Heidi followed their excited son and daughter.

"Gordon, you're going to live on a farm!" Eva announced.

The goat looked up in surprise from his supper of oats and barley.

Karl, Heidi and Mark linked arms and watched quietly.

But Eva clapped her hands and jumped up and down. "Rusty has found his family and Gordon's got a new home," she said. "Wow, is this a great day, or what!"